W9-BAM-997

4 Beloved Tales

HANSEL AND GRETEL

Stories Around the World

by Cari Meister

PICTURE WINDOW BOOKS
a capstone imprint

What Is a Fairy Tale?

Once upon a time, before the age of books, people gathered to tell stories. They told tales of fairies and magic, princes and witches. Ideas of love, jealousy, kindness, and luck filled the stories. Some provided lessons. Others just entertained. Most did both! These fairy tales passed from neighbor to neighbor, village to village, land to land. As the stories spun across seas and over mountains, details changed to fit each culture. A poisoned apple became a poisoned ring. A king became a sultan. A wolf became a tiger.

Over time, fairy tales were collected and written down. Around the world today, people of all ages love to read or hear these timeless stories. For many years to come, fairy tales will continue to live happily ever after in our imaginations.

HANSEL AND GRETEL
A GERMAN FAIRY TALE

illustrated by
Marina le Ray

Once there lived a poor woodcutter and his family. One year a famine spread throughout the land.

"We can no longer feed ourselves," said the woodcutter. "What shall we do?"

His wife replied, "Tomorrow we'll take Hansel and Gretel deep into the woods and leave them. We'll have two less mouths to feed."

The woodcutter was horrified, for he loved his children. But he didn't know what else to do.

The children had been listening through the wall. They had heard what their stepmother had said.

"Don't worry, Gretel," said Hansel. "I'll save us."

Hansel crept outside and stuffed his pockets with bright white rocks.

In the morning their father walked them deep into the woods. Hansel dropped the rocks behind them, one by one.

Far in the woods, the woodcutter made a fire. "Rest here," he said.

Soon the children were asleep.

At midnight they woke up and their father was gone. But Hansel's rocks shone a path in the moonlight. The children followed the rocks. By morning they were home.

Their stepmother was furious. That night she told her husband, "We must try again tomorrow." Then she bolted the door so Hansel could not collect rocks.

In the morning Hansel shoved a piece of bread in his pocket. As they walked, Hansel dropped breadcrumbs.

Again, the woodcutter made a fire, and the children fell asleep. When they woke, their father was gone, but this time there was no path. Birds had eaten the bread!

Poor Hansel and Gretel! They wandered through the woods with nothing to eat but a few berries. On the third day, a bird appeared and led them to a little house made of sugar.

"The roof is cake!" exclaimed Hansel. "The windows are sugar!"

As the children feasted, an old woman hobbled out. "Nibble, nibble, little mouse," she said. "Who is nibbling at my house?"

The old woman invited the children in and made them pancakes with honey. Then she put them to bed. Little did the children know, she was really a witch!

The next morning she locked Hansel in a cage. "I shall eat you," she said. "But first I'll fatten you up!"

Several days later the witch decided it was time to eat Hansel. She put wood in the oven to make it nice and hot. "Gretel," she said, "get into the oven and tell me if it's hot enough."

"I don't understand," lied Gretel. "Show me."

"You fool!" cried the witch. "You crawl in, like this—"

When the witch was halfway in the oven, Gretel shoved her and locked the latch. The witch howled. And then it was quiet.

Gretel found the key to the cage and set Hansel free. The two of them raced back to their home.

When their father saw them, he was overjoyed, for he had been heartbroken without them. *As for their stepmother ... she had already died.*

THE WITCH
A RUSSIAN FAIRY TALE

illustrated by
Kristina Swarner

Long ago a man had twins—a boy and a girl. His loving wife died, so he remarried. Sadly, his new wife detested the twins and wanted them gone.

"I know," she thought. "I'll send them to the witch!"

One day she looked at the children and said, "Go and work for my granny. She lives in a hut in the woods."

Along the way, the twins stopped at their own grandmother's house.

"Your stepmother is sending you to the witch!" cried their grandmother. "I can do nothing but give you this ham and bread. Be kind. You may be saved."

Later that day the twins found the hut. They knocked on the door.

A raggedy old witch opened the door. "Yes?" she snarled.

Trembling, the twins replied, "We're here to work for you."

"Very well," said the witch. "If I'm pleased with you, you'll live. If not, I'll eat you!"

She gave the girl a spinning wheel. "Spin!" she demanded. Then she vanished.

The girl began to sob.

Suddenly, hundreds of mice appeared. "Sweet child with eyes so red," they said. "If you need help, give us some bread."

So the girl gave them bread, and they spun for the witch.

The witch gave the boy a sieve. "Use this to fill my bathtub," she demanded.

The boy tried his impossible task, but water kept leaking from the sieve.

Suddenly, a flock of wrens landed. "This task you will not dread," they said. "If you need help, give us some bread."

The boy sprinkled breadcrumbs for the hungry wrens.

"Fill the holes with clay," they said. "Then draw the water. It'll stay."

And it did.

As the girl and boy were watching the animals finish their tasks, a cat wandered over. "If you have some ham for me," she purred. "I shall help set you free."

The children started feeding the cat their ham. "Dear Pussycat," they said, "how can we be set free?"

"Here's a handkerchief and comb," purred Pussycat. "If the witch follows you, throw them—"

Just then the witch clomped up the steps. "I see you've finished your tasks," she grumbled. "I guess I can't eat you today."

The next morning before the witch woke up, the children escaped. They passed the watchdog by giving him the rest of the bread.

When the witch discovered they were gone, she threw a shoe at Pussycat. "Why didn't you scratch their eyes out?"

"In 12 years you've never given me a scrap," replied Pussycat. "They gave me ham."

She turned to the dog. "Why didn't you bite them?" she asked.

"In 12 years you've never given me a scrap," replied the dog. "They gave me bread."

"Fools!" she yelled, running after the twins.

When the boy saw her, he threw the handkerchief. *A roaring river appeared.* It slowed the witch, but it didn't stop her.

The girl threw the comb. *A dense forest appeared.* Try as she might, the witch couldn't get through.

The twins ran all the way home. When they told their father what had happened, he sent the stepmother away for good.

Nennillo and Nennella
An Italian Fairy Tale

illustrated by
Alida Massari

There is an old Italian saying:

*A good stepmother
is like a white crow.*

Nennillo and Nennella lived
with their father, Jannuccio,
and their crazy stepmother. One day their stepmother
convinced Jannuccio to get rid of them. So Jannuccio filled a
basket with delicious food. He took his children by the hand
and led them deep into the forest.

"My loves," he said. "Your stepmother is like a diseased boar.
The woods will take better care of you than she will. Drink clean
water from the river. Sleep on the soft grass. If you ever need
anything, just follow the trail of grain I have left. I will get you
what you need." With a heavy heart, he turned and left.

Nennillo and Nennella played in the woods and ate the delicious food. But soon it got dark. The river made frightening noises, terrifying the children. They looked for the trail of grain, but a donkey had eaten it.

The children wandered in the forest for days. They were cold, hungry, and scared. One afternoon they heard the sound of hunting hounds. Poor Nennella was so terrified she ran until she reached the sea. There, she stumbled upon a pirate. The pirate's daughter had recently died, so he took Nennella home to his wife where she was raised as their own.

Nennillo did not follow Nennella to the sea.
Instead, he jumped into the first hollow tree.
A prince who was the leader of the hunters found
him. The prince, filled with pity, took Nennillo
back to his castle and raised him to be kind.

Four years passed.

Then one day as the pirate's family was sailing, a giant wave overturned their boat.

Nennella was the only survivor. As she splashed in the sea, a giant fish swallowed her. The fish swam toward a rock near the prince's castle. It just so happened that Nennillo was standing on the castle's balcony at that exact moment.

"Brother!" cried Nennella from the fish's mouth.

Nennillo and the prince ran to the rock, and the brother and sister were reunited. They told the prince their sad tale.

The prince spread the word, and soon Jannuccio
and the stepmother arrived at the castle.

"My children!" said Jannuccio kissing them. "I thought
you were eaten by wolves. I've lived every day
in heartache! Please forgive me."

As for the stepmother, the prince put her in a barrel and sent her rolling over the mountain.

She was last heard saying, "One who mischief seeks, shall to mischief fall; There comes an hour that pays for all."

JUAN AND MARIA
A FAIRY TALE FROM
THE PHILIPPINES illustrated by Teresa Ramos

Once upon a time, in a poor barrio, lived a family. The father was very lazy and did not work. The only food the family ate was what the father begged for. One day he came home with a small handful of rice. But when the wife cooked it, the husband grew furious.

"There is never enough!" he screamed. "Chase our children away. They will have to find their own food."

Little Juan and Maria were sent into the wild forest alone.

"My tummy rumbles," cried Maria.

Juan looked around. Good fortune smiled down. Juan found a guava tree with one lone fruit. "Here, Maria," he said. "Eat this."

As they walked Maria found a hen's egg. She put it in her pocket. Soon they came to a small hut covered in long, dry grass called talahib.

A kind woman invited them in. When she learned what had happened, she said, "You can stay here. I'll treat you like my own children."

A few days later, the hen's egg hatched into a rooster. It became Maria's constant companion.

Years passed, and Maria grew into a beautiful woman. Juan became a strong, kind man. He spent much of his time hunting in the woods. One morning he spotted a fine black deer.

"Once you've finished eating me, put my skin in your trunk," said the deer. "In three days open your trunk. You will find a gift."

Juan obeyed. When he opened his trunk on the third day, he found a golden suit of armor.

Around the same time, Maria's rooster began to talk. "Tok-toko-kok! I'm ready to fight!" it crowed.

The next Sunday Juan took the rooster to fight in a local contest. To his astonishment, the rooster won. Juan returned home with a maletin of money.

Not too much later, a proclamation went out from the king's palace:

The princess needs a husband. Whoever wins my tournament
will inherit the throne and my daughter's hand.

Juan immediately set out for the palace. As fate would have it, he won the tournament. He married the princess and later took the throne.

As for Maria ...

Shortly thereafter, she found a prince lost in the woods.
He fell instantly in love with her. The two were married.

Maria and Juan wanted to know what had happened to their
parents. Maria and Juan found them wretched and hungry.

"I beg your forgiveness, your majesties," cried their father.
"I treated you cruelly."

Because Juan and Maria had kind hearts, they forgave their
parents. They made sure their parents lived their remaining
years without want.

GLOSSARY

barrio—a neighborhood where Spanish is the main language

boar—a wild pig

detest—to dislike very much

famine—a serious shortage of food resulting in widespread hunger and death

furious—very mad

maletin—a satchel or bag

sieve—a container consisting of wire or plastic mesh in a frame, used for separating large pieces from small pieces or liquids from solids

CRITICAL THINKING WITH COMMON CORE

1. Look at the illustrations for "The Witch." What details tell you the story takes place in Russia? (Key Ideas and Details)

2. Pick one theme in the stories such as "forgiveness." Explain how it varies in each story. (Integration of Knowledge and Ideas)

3. How are the stepmothers and mothers portrayed in the stories? Why were they described in that way? (Key Ideas and Details)

WRITING PROMPTS

1. Which house in the woods would you like to visit? Why?

2. If you were Juan or Maria, would you go back and help your parents? Explain your reasoning.

3. Write your own modern-day Hansel and Gretel story.

Read More

Gaiman, Neil & Mattotti, Lorenzo. *Hansel & Gretel.* New York: Toon Graphics, 2014.

Hobbie, Holly. *Hansel and Gretel.* Boston: Little Brown Books for Young Readers, 2015.

Isadora, Rachel. *Hansel and Gretel.* New York: Putnam, 2009.

North, Laura. *Hansel and Gretel and the Green Witch.* Ontario, Canada: Crabtree, 2015.

Internet Sites

FactHound offers a safe, fun way to find Internet sites related to this book. All of the sites on FactHound have been researched by our staff.

Here's all you do:

Visit *www.facthound.com*

Type in this code: 9781479597062

Super-cool stuff! Check out projects, games and lots more at www.capstonekids.com

Thanks to our adviser for her expertise and advice:
Maria Tatar, PhD, Chair, Program in Folklore & Mythology

Editor: Penny West
Designer: Ashlee Suker
Creative Director: Nathan Gassman
Production Specialist: Laura Manthe

Picture Window Books are published by Capstone,
1710 Roe Crest Drive, North Mankato, Minnesota 56003
www.mycapstone.com

Library of Congress Cataloging-in-Publication Data
Names: Meister, Cari, author.
Title: Hansel and Gretel stories around the world : 4 beloved tales/ by Cari Meister.
Other titles: Nonfiction picture books. Multicultural fairy tales
Description: North Mankato, Minnesota : Capstone Press, [2017]
Series: Nonfiction picture books. Multicultural fairy tales | Summary: Retells the classic Grimm fairy tale of the children who encounter a witch in the forest, together with three similar tales from Russia, Italy, and the Philippines. | Includes bibliographical references.
Identifiers: LCCN 2015050457
ISBN 9781479597062 (library binding)
ISBN 9781515804154 (pbk.)
ISBN 9781515804239 (ebook (pdf))
Subjects: LCSH: Hansel and Gretel (Tale) | Fairy tales. | Folklore. CYAC: Fairy tales. | Folklore.
Classification: LCC PZ8.M5183 Han 2017 | DDC 398.209—dc23
LC record available at http://lccn.loc.gov/2015050457

3 1907 00368 8172

Printed in the United States of America.
009688F16

Look for other the books in the series: